A Note to Parents and Caregivers:

Read-it! Readers are for children who are just starting on the amazing road to reading. These beautiful books support both the acquisition of reading skills and the love of books.

 The PURPLE LEVEL presents basic topics and objects using high frequency words and simple language patterns.

 The RED LEVEL presents familiar topics using common words and repeating sentence patterns.

 The BLUE LEVEL presents new ideas using a larger vocabulary and varied sentence structure.

 The YELLOW LEVEL presents more challenging ideas, a broad vocabulary, and wide variety in sentence structure.

 The GREEN LEVEL presents more complex ideas, an extended vocabulary range, and expanded language structures.

 The ORANGE LEVEL presents a wide range of ideas and concepts using challenging vocabulary and complex language structures.

When sharing a book with your child, read in short stretches, pausing often to talk about the pictures. Have your child turn the pages and point to the pictures and familiar words. And be sure to reread favorite stories or parts of stories.

There is no right or wrong way to share books with children. Find time to read with your child, and pass on the legacy of literacy.

Adria F. Klein, Ph.D.
Professor Emeritus
California State University
San Bernardino, California

Editor: Christianne Jones
Designer: Amy Bailey Muehlenhardt
Page Production: Tracy Kaehler
Creative Director: Keith Griffin
Editorial Director: Carol Jones
The illustrations in this book were created digitally.

Picture Window Books
5115 Excelsior Boulevard
Suite 232
Minneapolis, MN 55416
877-845-8392
www.picturewindowbooks.com

Printed in the United States of America.

Library of Congress Cataloging-in-Publication Data
Dougherty, Terri.
The best lunch / by Terri Dougherty ; illustrated by Patrick Kouse.
p. cm. — (Read-it! readers)
Summary: A lunchroom accident which ruins Kendra's anticipated meal of nachos has
an unexpected outcome.
ISBN 1-4048-1578-3 (hardcover)
[1. Schools—Fiction. 2. Food—Fiction.] I. Kouse, Patrick, ill. II. Title. III. Series.

PZ7.D74436Bes 2005
[E]—dc22   2005021442

The Best Lunch

by Terri Dougherty
illustrated by Patrick Kouse

Special thanks to our advisers for their expertise:

Adria F. Klein, Ph.D.
Professor Emeritus, California State University
San Bernardino, California

Susan Kesselring, M.A.
Literacy Educator
Rosemount–Apple Valley–Eagan (Minnesota) School District

CANCEL

PICTURE WINDOW BOOKS
Minneapolis, Minnesota

It was nachos day at school. Kendra couldn't wait for lunch! At noon, she lined up with her class and headed toward the lunchroom.

4

5

Kendra made sure she put her toy dinosaur, Chip, in her pocket.

He went everywhere with her.

Our Camping Trip

Kendra watched the cook add cheese to her nacho cup. Kendra placed Chip on the front of her tray.

Just then, Jack bumped into her.

"Ouch!" Kendra yelled.

Nachos splattered all over the floor.

Kendra got a broom and rag and
cleaned up the mess.

By the time Kendra was done cleaning up, only peanut butter and jelly sandwiches were left.

"What could be worse?" she thought.

Kendra looked for a place to sit, but all of the tables were full.

16

The only spot left was next to Jack.

"Here's an open seat," said Jack.

"Thanks," she said. "Just my luck. My milk won't open."

"Could this lunch get any worse?" Kendra cried.

"It seems like you are having a bad day. Can I make things better?" asked Jack.

"Only if you want to trade lunches," said Kendra.

"Sure," said Jack.

"Thanks!" Kendra said. "I've got to show Chip my new lunch." But when she looked in her pocket, Chip wasn't there.

"Oh, no! I've lost my dinosaur!" Kendra yelled.

"Does it look like this?" asked Jack, pulling a dinosaur from his pocket.

"It's Chip!" Kendra cheered.

"I found him on the floor after I bumped into you," Jack said. "I'm really sorry about that."

Kendra looked at Chip and smiled. Then she smiled at Jack.

"That's OK," she said. "I found two friends today. What could be better?"

More *Read-it!* Readers

Bright pictures and fun stories help you practice your reading skills. Look for more books at your level.

Bamboo at the Beach 1-4048-1035-8

Clinks the Robot 1-4048-1579-1

The Crying Princess 1-4048-0053-0

Eight Enormous Elephants 1-4048-0054-9

Flynn Flies High 1-4048-0563-X

Freddie's Fears 1-4048-0056-5

Loop, Swoop, and Pull! 1-4048-1611-9

Marvin, the Blue Pig 1-4048-0564-8

Mary and the Fairy 1-4048-0066-2

Megan Has to Move 1-4048-1613-5

Moo! 1-4048-0643-1

My Favorite Monster 1-4048-1029-3

Pippin's Big Jump 1-4048-0555-9

Pony Party 1-4048-1612-7

The Queen's Dragon 1-4048-0553-2

Sounds Like Fun 1-4048-0649-0

Tired of Waiting 1-4048-0650-4

Whose Birthday Is It? 1-4048-0554-0

Looking for a specific title or level? A complete list of *Read-it!* Readers is available on our Web site:
www.picturewindowbooks.com